DATE DUE

SEP 1 2 2005			
OCT 1 1 2005			

D0961367

DEMCO 38-297

HERBIE JONES AND THE CLASS GIFT

If Annabelle Louisa Hodgekiss hadn't suggested the end-of-the-year gift for their third grade teacher, Herbie Jones and his best friend Raymond Martin wouldn't be in this mess. Miss Perfect Annabelle said that every kid in the class had to kick in one dollar for the present, or they didn't get to sign the card. And Herbie and Ray just don't have the money. Fortunately, ingenious Herbie figures out a way to earn the money. Unfortunately, Raymond figures out a way to eat up all the profits. But with Herbie Jones leading the way, they come through with the cash—and more trouble than they bargained for. With the terrible twosome in charge, will Miss Pinkham and the whole third grade class ever see their present?

"Hapless Herbie is back with his troublemaking friend Ray for one last third-grade adventure before school is out....This is a heartfelt, funny story to add to the growing Herbie Jones titles, a list that is still too short for the ingenuous third grader's fans."
—*Publishers Weekly*

Herbie Jones
and the Class Gift

by Suzy Kline

illustrated by Richard Williams

Puffin Books

Acknowledgments

Special thanks to Nancy-Jo Hereford and
Jane Schall for the idea of a class gift.
And as always, special appreciation to my
editor, Anne O'Connell, and my husband, Rufus.
Thanks for your interest and insights.
To Jennifer, Emily, Mom and Nancy,
thanks for being you.

PUFFIN BOOKS
A Division of Penguin Books USA Inc.
375 Hudson Street, New York, New York 10014
Penguin Books Ltd, 27 Wrights Lane, London W8 5TZ, England
Penguin Books Australia Ltd, Ringwood, Victoria, Australia
Penguin Books Canada Ltd, 10 Alcorn Avenue, Toronto, Ontario, Canada M4V 3B2
Penguin Books (N.Z.) Ltd, 182–190 Wairau Road, Auckland 10, New Zealand

Penguin Books Ltd, Registered Offices: Harmondsworth, Middlesex, England

First published in the United States of America by G.P. Putnam's Sons, 1987
Published in Puffin Books 1989
13 15 17 19 20 18 16 14
Text copyright © Suzy Kline, 1987   Illustrations copyright © Richard Williams, 1987
All rights reserved

LIBRARY OF CONGRESS CATALOGING-IN-PUBLICATION DATA

Kline, Suzy.   Herbie Jones and the class gift.
Reprint. Originally published: New York: Putnam's, 1987.
Summary: Disaster strikes when Annabelle trusts Herbie Jones
and Raymond with the job of picking up the class's gift to their teacher.
[1. Schools—Fiction. 2. Gifts—Fiction.
3. Humorous stories] I. Williams, Richard, ill. II. Title.
PZ7.K6797Hg 1989 [Fic] 88-30556 ISBN 0-14-032723-1

Printed in the United States of America

Set in Caledonia

Dedicated with Love to
My Students

Keep Reading and Writing!

◄ Contents ►

Herbie Jones
and the Class Gift

The Class Gift

Herbie Jones hated indoor recess.

Especially in June.

As he looked out his classroom window and listened to the rain, he thought about the night crawlers coming to the top of his lawn. It would be easy to get some tonight for fishing bait.

Herbie looked over at his best friend Raymond Martin. He was busy drawing Viking ships.

Just as Herbie pulled out a book to read, Annabelle Louisa Hodgekiss walked up to the front of the room and clapped her hands three times like she was the teacher.

"I want everyone's attention," she said firmly.

Herbie noticed her reddish-brown hair was tied up in pigtails. He liked the dolphin on her T-shirt.

"I'm waiting for Raymond Martin," she said, flaring her nostrils.

Raymond put down his purple crayon and made a face.

"I have something very important to say," Annabelle began, "and I am telling you now because the teacher is out of the room."

"Ooooh . . ." Herbie replied, "TOP SECRET!"

Annabelle raised her eyebrows. "Are you through *ooh*ing, Herbie Jones?"

Herbie nodded. He half-wondered what she was going to say.

"The last day of school many of us give Miss Pinkham a gift, like a coffee cup or . . ."

"Some fudge . . ." John Greenweed interrupted. "I even make it myself."

Sarah Sitwellington joined in, "I was painting 'WORLD'S BEST TEACHER' on a piece of wood."

"Well," Annabelle continued, "I think we should do things differently this year."

"Me too," Raymond agreed. "I don't think we have to give her anything."

Annabelle flared her nostrils again.

"We could make one big class card," Herbie suggested, "and have everybody sign it."

"A card isn't enough, Herbie. But we would need one. You could write a poem for it."

Herbie was getting impatient. "So what is YOUR big idea?"

Annabelle cleared her throat. "I was thinking we could all chip in a dollar and get Miss Pinkham one big class gift."

Ray leaned back in his chair, "I like Herbie's card idea. It's cheaper. I'm a bit short this time of year."

"You're ALWAYS short, Raymond Martin."

Ray tipped back too far and fell off his chair.

"Well," John said, "maybe a class gift is okay, but who would pick it out?"

Annabelle sat down on a desk the way the teacher did. "Me," she said.

"You?" John objected. "How come YOU get to pick it out?"

Annabelle folded her arms, "Because *I* have seen the inside of Miss Pinkham's house."

"You have?" The class looked interested.

"That was last month when I delivered some chocolate mint Girl Scout cookies. I happen to know Miss Pinkham collects ceramic owls. And I saw a beautiful ceramic owl at Martha's House of Gifts on Main Street for just twenty-four sixty-seven, including tax."

"Twenty-four dollars?" Ray shouted. "Man, that's a lot of moola!"

"Not if we each contribute one dollar," Annabelle replied.

John Greenweed counted heads. "We have twenty-eight people in our class. You would be collecting twenty-eight dollars."

"I don't expect some people to pay," Annabelle said, eyeballing Raymond.

"Wait a minute," Herbie broke in, "I think Ray has a point. Twenty-four dollars IS a lot of money. My dad always said the best gifts are the ones you make yourself, like . . . John's fudge and Sarah's sign."

"Right on," Ray said, climbing back into his chair. "Gifts from the liver are the best kind."

The class turned quiet.

"GIFTS FROM THE LIVER?" Annabelle said. "Aaaaauuugh! You mean gifts from the HEART."

And then everyone laughed.

When they were through, Herbie spoke up.

"Listen you guys, the liver and heart are practically next to each other. It's like saying the same thing."

Ray beamed. He liked it when Herbie stuck up for him.

Margie Sherman raised her hand. "I'm tired of talking about hearts and livers. I like the owl gift. And Annabelle said Miss Pinkham collects them."

Herbie rolled his eyes. Naturally Margie would go along with Annabelle. They were best friends.

"I make a motion that we accept Annabelle's idea to bring in one dollar for Miss Pinkham's end-of-the-year gift," Margie finished.

". . . by Friday," Annabelle prompted.

". . . by Friday," Margie repeated.

"Is there a second?" Annabelle said.

"You want to buy TWO?" Herbie asked.

Annabelle ignored him. "All in favor, say 'aye,'" she called.

"AYE."

"Opposed, say 'nay.'"

Herbie and Raymond shouted, "Say nay."

"A simple 'nay' is sufficient," Annabelle said coldly. Then she recorded the votes at the chalkboard. "Twenty-six to two." She beamed. "The majority wins! We will get Miss Pinkham one big class gift." After a short pause, Annabelle lowered her eyebrows. "I will start collecting your dollars tomorrow."

"*And* we will need a card," she continued. "Herbie, could you write a poem for it?"

Herbie half-nodded. He was looking at the book on his desk.

"Of course, I'll have to recopy it for neatness. Just get the poem to me in the next few days. I'll make sure the ONLY people who sign our card are the ones who paid."

Raymond picked up his purple crayon and went back to coloring his Viking ship.

Herbie kept on reading.

After school Herbie and Ray walked home in the drizzling rain. It felt good on such a hot day.

"Annabelle is so bossy," Raymond said. "She always gets her way."

"Always," Herbie agreed. Then he bent down and picked up a night crawler off the sidewalk. "We can fish with this on Saturday."

Raymond didn't bother looking at the worm.

"Can you loan me a dollar for that owl?" he blurted out. "I don't want to be the only person not signing the class card. Miss Pinkham's nice. She says I draw real good."

Herbie dropped the worm and looked at his pal. The rain was dripping down Ray's face and onto his yellow T-shirt.

"You're really worried about this class gift business, aren't you?"

Ray put his hands in his pockets. "You're lucky, Herbie, both your parents work and they get along. My dad, well, he got laid off last week, and things haven't been very good. My parents argue a lot about money."

Herbie knew that Mr. Martin was a janitor somewhere. He felt bad about his losing a job. He was glad his dad still worked the nightshift at Northeastern. That was a place that made airplane seats.

"Listen Ray, I can *give* you a dollar."

"You can?"

"Sure, come on! Let's go to my house for the money."

2

The Roof Caves In!

As Herbie walked into the kitchen, Mr. Jones was sitting at the table drinking from his coffee mug. He was also looking at the day's mail.

"Hi, Dad," Herbie said. "Where's Olive?" That was the nickname Herbie had for his sister, Olivia.

Mr. Jones wrinkled his face. "She's shopping with your mother."

"Oh." Herbie remembered Wednesday was his mom's day off. Usually she worked at Dipping Donuts from seven o'clock in the morning till five o'clock at night. Unless it was Sunday. Then she went to work after church.

Herbie knew shopping trips put his dad in a bad mood. It meant more bills.

Herbie decided to ask about the two dollars a little later.

"Chocolate frosted or jelly?" Herbie asked Ray as he peeked in the purple bag on the table. That was the best part about having his mom work at a donut place, Herbie thought. She brought home free day-old donuts.

"Chocolate," Ray replied.

Ray sat down at the table. After he finished the chocolate donut he reached for the purple bag. "Think I'll try that jelly one, now."

Herbie shook his head. Ray ALWAYS had to have seconds.

"Sorry to hear about your dad," Mr. Jones said as he sipped from his mug. "Times are hard. You just gotta hang on to your money."

"Yeah," Ray said. "I try to borrow from other people. That way I'm spending their money and not mine."

Herbie started to cough. He got up to get some milk from the refrigerator.

"No milk?" he said.

"Nope," Mr. Jones grumbled, "no coffee either. You boys will have to drink what I'm drinking."

Herbie and Ray immediately leaned over the table and looked into Mr. Jones's cup.

"What's that?" Ray asked.

"Adam's Ale."

"Adam what? Looks like water to me," Herbie replied.

"It is," Mr. Jones agreed. "That's exactly what Adam and Eve drank. Now, it's the world's most popular drink. Least expensive, too."

Herbie and Ray looked at each other and made a face.

"WE'RE HOME!" Mrs. Jones shouted as Olivia rushed into the kitchen with two big grocery bags.

Herbie grabbed the milk. He was thirsty.

"Oh Dad, I found the most gorgeous, outstanding dress in the world."

Mr. Jones drummed his fingers on the table. "How outstanding is the price?"

"We put it on layaway, Dad, and each week I'm adding my babysitting money along with yours."

"I don't babysit," Mr. Jones mumbled.

Mrs. Jones sank into a kitchen chair. Her high heels were hurting her feet, so she took one off and set it on her lap. "Henry," she said, "let me explain why we are getting the dress in the first place."

"Yes. . . ?"

"Olivia has been asked to give a speech at the

English Honor Society Banquet, and I thought, well . . . she should wear something extra nice."

Herbie knew his mom was big on English. She had studied it at Laurel Woods Community College. When Olivia wasn't correcting his speech, his mother was.

"And just how much was Olivia's dress?" Mr. Jones's voice got louder as he spoke.

"I'll tell you, Henry, when . . . you lower your voice."

Ray raised his eyebrows as he watched Herbie pour them some milk. He had never seen the Joneses argue about money before.

"It's lowered," Mr. Jones replied.

Mrs. Jones looked down as she ran her finger along the edge of the shoe she was holding. "Forty-five dollars," she said softly.

"FORTY-FIVE DOLLARS!" Now Mr. Jones's voice roared. He pounded the table with his fist so hard, the purple bag of donuts jumped an inch.

"Why, for FORTY-FIVE-DOLLARS I could fix our cracked ceiling and make it look like new!"

Olivia started to cry. "What's more important, Dad—me, or some dumb old ceiling?"

"In this case, it's easy. The ceiling."

Raymond tried not to laugh. He knew it wasn't funny.

Olivia stormed out of the kitchen and slammed the door so hard a piece of plaster fell from the ceiling. It landed in the middle of the table.

"Man," Ray shouted, "Look at that! Some meteor, huh, Herbie?"

Herbie picked it up and looked at it.

"*Now*, Mary," Mr. Jones continued, "WHICH do you think is more important? A dress for one night, or a ceiling that's caving in on us?"

Mrs. Jones stood up from the table and started waving the shoe that was in her hand. "Henry Jones, you are the biggest tightwad I know. Sometimes you have to splurge a little in life. You're acting like a . . . like a . . ."

Ray looked at the red shoe she was waving in the air and smiled. "A high heel?" He wanted to be helpful.

Mr. Jones leaned over the table and whispered, "You mean *heel*, Raymond." Then he couldn't help but laugh.

Mrs. Jones threw down her shoe. "I don't think this is one bit funny!" Then she clomped out of the kitchen with one shoe on and one shoe off.

"Well," Mr. Jones called out after her, "I think I'm just being practical. My mother always said 'A penny saved is a penny earned.' If you have to spend money, make sure it's for something you need."

Herbie knew the timing wasn't right now to ask his father for ANYTHING.

"Come on, Ray," Herbie said, "I'll walk you to the porch."

When they got outside, Ray said, "Man, Herbie, I feel a lot better about things."

"You do?"

"I didn't know your parents argue about money too."

Herbie shrugged. He didn't either.

"At least I know my dad loves me more than my kitchen ceiling," Ray said with a toothy smile.

Herbie shook his head. "My dad didn't mean that. He's just worried about money."

Then Herbie had a sinking feeling. If his dad was worried about money how could he ever ask him for the two dollars?

3

Annabelle
Is After School

In class the next day, Miss Pinkham said, "Boys and girls, today we are going to learn about different states of matter."

Herbie sat up. He liked science.

"We're going to see how a solid can change to a liquid when heat is added to it."

The class watched Miss Pinkham walk to the door. Herbie thought she had the longest legs he had ever seen. She always walked fast.

"Now, I am going to get some things from the school refrigerator. While I am gone for one minute, I expect all of you to STAY IN YOUR SEATS."

The class nodded.

As soon as Miss Pinkham left the room, Annabelle scooted up the aisle and spoke to the class.

"So far, I have collected eighteen dollars for Miss Pinkham's gift. I want the rest of the money by tomorrow—that's Friday . . . the day we agreed upon. So, be sure to bring . . ."

Herbie looked over at the doorway. Miss Pinkham was standing there with two trays of ice cubes and a surprised look on her face.

"Annabelle Louisa Hodgekiss! Of all people, *you* are the one out of your seat. There must be some good explanation for it."

Herbie wondered if Annabelle was going to spill the beans about the class gift.

So did everyone else.

It was pin quiet.

Annabelle shook her head and walked back to her seat.

"Well," Miss Pinkham continued, "I can't make exceptions to our classroom rules. You will have to . . . stay after school."

The class gasped.

Annabelle Louisa Hodgekiss had never been after school in her life!

Raymond leaned forward on his elbows and smiled.

Herbie looked at Annabelle's face as she returned to her seat. It was as red as her ribbons.

He knew this was an historic moment. Annabelle after school! He looked at the date, June twelfth. He would remember it.

Raymond raised his hand, "Doesn't she have to write something one hundred times, and sweep the floor, and clap erasers, and wash the blackboards and dust the desktop and straighten the bookshelves?"

Ray would know the punishment better than anyone else, Herbie thought.

"Ah . . . yes . . . uh, that's true. Annabelle, you will need to write, 'I will not leave my seat.'"

Ray was disappointed. He knew if it had been *him* out of his seat, she would have had him write a longer sentence. Something like: "I will not leave my seat when the teacher is out of the room to get ice cubes."

Annabelle took a lined sheet of paper from her binder and one of her pencils that had her initials, ALH, in gold.

Then she began writing.

Neatly.

Herbie couldn't see her face now, but he did see some tears dropping on her paper.

He had never seen Annabelle cry before.

Herbie began to wonder if the punishment was fair. After all, she was doing something nice for the teacher. And because she wanted to keep the class gift a secret, she was willing to stay after school.

Herbie thought about his money problem and wondered what *he* was willing to do. Giving the teacher a class gift *was* a nice idea. And it was important. He didn't have to get the two dollars from his dad. He and Ray could earn it themselves. After school.

As the boys walked across the school lawn, Ray kept saying, "Annabelle Louisa Hodgekiss is after school! Yahoo! Yahoo!"

"Come on, Ray," Herbie complained. "We've got business to take care of. We have to earn two dollars this afternoon."

"Yeah . . . but we still have time for one peek."

"One peek where?"

"At Annabelle. If we climb the big maple we can see her through the windows."

"How boring," Herbie replied. "Who wants to look at her?"

"Listen Herbie, right after we take ONE PEEK, we can go straight to my house and wash bottles like you said, and get five cents a piece for them. All we need is twenty bottles."

"Forty bottles," Herbie corrected, "and that's a lot of washing. Let's not waste time spying on Annabelle."

"Just one peek?" Ray persisted.

"ALL RIGHT!" Herbie was bugged. He grabbed the lowest branch and then shimmied up the tree. Ray followed close behind.

As the boys crawled out on the branch closest to their classroom window, they could see Annabelle.

"Now . . ." whispered Herbie, "What's so great about that? She's just washing the blackboards with a yellow sponge. Big deal."

Ray didn't say anything, he just kept staring at Annabelle. "Boy, doesn't that make you feel good, to watch HER wash those boards?"

Herbie shook his head.

Then he noticed something else.

Miss Pinkham was at her desk. While Annabelle's back was to her, the teacher reached into a bottom drawer and took out a tube of lipstick, a comb and a mirror.

Herbie's eyes widened as he watched *his teacher* put on lipstick and comb her hair.

"Isn't this great?" Ray said as he kept his eyes glued to Annabelle.

"Yeah . . ." Herbie replied, watching Miss Pinkham rub her lips together and then blot them on a lunch slip! A LUNCH SLIP!

"Okay, we can go now," Ray said, dropping to the lawn below.

Herbie was still staring at his teacher.

"Come on, Herbie, come on."

"Just a second . . ." Herbie said. He saw Miss Pinkham check to see if Annabelle's back was still turned.

Then she stood up and aimed for the waste-paper basket clear across the room. Herbie watched the piece of crumpled paper fly high in the air, hit the wall, and then rebound into the basket.

Miss Pinkham kicked her leg up high, smiled,

and gave the thumbs up sign!

Herbie grinned.

He'd seen it all.

He also knew if anyone else had done that in class, they would be after school for sure!

"Come on," Ray prodded. "Let's go wash bottles."

Herbie dropped down to the grass beside his buddy.

"So," Ray said, "you thought it was interesting too."

Herbie nodded.

"Very." He smiled.

4

Price Busters

"Gee, Ray," Herbie said as he squirted the hose into a Coke bottle. "Where have these been?"

Ray looked at the forty bottles they had lugged up from the basement and out to Ray's backyard. "They've been around."

"Look at the ants on this one," Herbie said.

"Just keep squirting 'em. Price Busters says they have to be clean."

"What's this?" Herbie said as he held up two bottles. "Yahoo Cola and Rooty Tooty Root Beer? My dad said they don't make these anymore. We won't get a nickel for 'em."

"So, I'll go down to the basement and get some more Coke bottles."

Herbie was impressed.

After an hour, the boys had washed forty bottles. Since most of them were two liters, they had to use four garbage sacks to carry them.

"Let's make like Santa Claus and head for Price Busters!" Herbie said with a smile.

He felt good. He and Ray were earning two dollars themselves and they would be part of things.

As the boys watched the grocery clerk at Price Busters total up the bottles, they discovered they were five cents over. The clerk handed Herbie two dollars and five cents.

"Can we have that nickel in five pennies?" Herbie asked.

The clerk nodded.

Herbie put the five pennies in the gum ball machine outside the store.

"Here, Ray, you can have the extra piece of gum. After all, they were your bottles."

Ray grinned as he popped a red, a yellow, and a white gum ball into his mouth.

"And you can take the two dollars to school tomorrow. Won't Annabelle be surprised to find out you have something more than burned-out fuses in your pockets!"

Ray beamed.

"I've got to get home fast and write that poem for the class card. See you tomorrow at the corner."

"See you tomorrow," Ray repeated.

5

Disaster
in Paradise!

The next day, Raymond was not at the corner. Herbie wondered what had happened to his buddy.

When he got to school, he found Ray leaning on the classroom door.

"Where were you?" Herbie asked.

Raymond didn't answer.

"What's up, Ray?"

Just then, Annabelle Louisa Hodgekiss came over to Herbie. He noticed she was wearing a sundress with strawberries all over it.

"Did you write the poem, Herbie?" she asked.

"Sure did," Herbie said as he reached into his back pocket. "Here."

Annabelle unfolded the paper and then read it aloud to several students who were standing near her.

This is a rhyme
At the end of the year
To say you are nice
    And sweet.
Enjoy your vacation —
Read some good books,
    Sit down and
    Put up your feet.

"I like it!" Annabelle said. "It rhymes and it's even spelled correctly."

Herbie was glad Olivia had checked the spelling for him.

"By the way," Annabelle continued, "I've collected twenty-four dollars for the gift so far. Don't you two want to contribute?"

"Sure do," Herbie grinned. "Right, Ray?"

Ray looked at Annabelle, and then walked away.

"Be back in a minute," Herbie said to Annabelle as he followed Ray to the pencil sharpener.

"What's the problem?"

"Remember yesterday when we said goodbye, and you went home and I went home . . ."

"Yeah . . ."

"Well, I sort of . . . took a short cut."

"So?"

" . . . by Burger Paradise."

"No. You didn't . . ."

"I smelled those cheeseburgers, Herbie, and I couldn't help myself. I *had* to go in."

"YOU SPENT OUR MONEY FOR MISS PINKHAM'S GIFT ON A CHEESEBURGER?"

"No," Ray replied. "On Bits O' Chicken."

"BITS O' CHICKEN?" Herbie shouted. "How could you do such a thing?"

"I was hungry so . . . I got the nine pack."

"You're ALWAYS hungry!"

" . . . with the barbecue sauce."

"Don't tell me any more!" Herbie said as he walked over to his desk and plopped in his chair.

Annabelle followed him. "You aren't giving anything?" she asked again.

Herbie shook his head.

"Well, it wouldn't be fair then if I let you sign the card. You haven't paid your dollar. Sorry."

Herbie looked outside the window at a squirrel climbing the maple tree. He couldn't wait till the three o'clock bell. He wanted to go home.

Alone.

He didn't think he would ever talk to Raymond Martin again.

Bits O' Chicken!

Herbie put his head down on his desk and closed his eyes.

When Herbie walked into his house, Olivia wasn't there. Probably babysitting again, he thought. His dad was snoring in the bedroom. Must have worked late, Herbie figured.

Herbie decided to walk to Dipping Donuts and see his mom.

When he got to the restaurant, he peeked through the glass at the clock that was in the shape of a donut. It said 4:15.

That meant Herbie had a forty-five–minute wait.

Herbie sat down on the curb in front of Dipping Donuts and watched the cars go by. Then he watched the birds fly by. Finally, he counted buses.

There were five of them.

At five o'clock, Herbie walked into the restaurant. His mother was just getting her sweater.

"What a nice surprise! You came to meet me?"

Herbie nodded.

"Want to come with me to Price Busters? I have to get a few groceries for the week."

Herbie shivered when she said the words "Price Busters." It reminded him of the two dollars.

Mrs. Jones lead Herbie out of Dipping Donuts. "Cat got your tongue?" she asked.

"Huh?"

"Don't you know what that means?"

Herbie shook his head. He wondered if he was going to get one of her English lessons.

"'Cat got your tongue' is a cliché."

"Clee-shay?"

"That's just a common expression like 'A piece of cake.' That means something is easy."

"Hmmmm," Herbie was trying to think of one.

"Like today," Mrs. Jones continued as she pushed a grocery cart into the store, "Mr. Pellizini kept yelling at me to do this and do that at the restaurant. I reminded myself that 'his bark is worse than his bite.' He doesn't hurt anyone. Or fire them. His voice just has an edge to it."

That made Herbie think of Annabelle. Her voice definitely had an edge to it. "Is 'A penny saved is a penny earned' one?"

Mrs. Jones put some potatoes in the cart.

"You've been talking to your father."

"And 'Spill the beans'?" Herbie asked.

"Both of them are. Very good, Herbie."

Herbie decided not to talk any more. He was thinking about the class gift again, and how Annabelle had kept it a secret.

"I still think you don't feel like talking. Something IS bothering you." Mrs. Jones stopped the cart by the lettuce. "What is it, Herbie?"

Herbie looked at his mom's brown eyes. He couldn't hold back his thoughts any more. It hurt too much.

So Herbie told his mother everything about the gift, the poem, the bottles and the Bits O' Chicken. And that it was too late.

"Well," Mrs. Jones replied when Herbie finished. "It isn't too late to give Annabelle the money."

"It isn't?"

"If you voted to pay her by Friday, you have all evening. It's still Friday."

Herbie snapped his fingers. Of course!

Mrs. Jones continued, "You can have the money as long as you and Olivia don't mind drinking Adam's Ale this week instead of soda."

"You know about Adam's Ale too?"

"I also talk to your father." Mrs. Jones half-smiled.

"Sure, Mom, sure!"

Herbie's eyes widened as he watched his mother open her brown purse and pull out two crisp dollar bills.

"Two? I just need one. Forget about old Bits O' Chicken Martin."

Mrs. Jones tried not to smile. "Herbie, Ray is your best friend. His dad is out of work. I'm giving you an extra dollar so Ray can sign the card, too. Here," she said. "You can stop by Annabelle's after dinner and take care of that class gift business."

Then she put her hands on his shoulders. "And when you write a poem, Herbie, make sure you put your name on it."

Herbie beamed.

He was so happy he thought about forgiving Raymond. Maybe, just maybe, he *might* ask Ray to go with him when he went to Annabelle's house.

And Herbie felt so happy he decided to do something he had never, ever, done in public before.

But first he looked both ways to make sure no one was around.

It was all clear so Herbie DID IT.

He gave his mother a big long hug.

Right there in Price Busters, in front of the tomatoes, the potatoes and the green beans.

6

Annabelle's Bark

Herbie and Ray rang the doorbell.

"I don't like Annabelle's house," Ray complained. "That Siamese cat doesn't look very friendly."

"Just remember what I said, Ray, Annabelle's bark isn't as bad as her bite."

"I'm not worried about HER bite right now. I'm worried about that cat's!"

Herbie rang the doorbell again. "Listen, Ray. You're lucky you're here. You shouldn't be complaining about anything. Not after what you did."

Ray didn't say anything more. He just moved closer to Herbie, and further away from the cat.

"Hi boys!" Mr. Hodgekiss said as he opened the door.

"Hello, Mr. Hodgekiss," Herbie replied. He noticed Annabelle's father was wearing a flowered apron. Probably Mrs. Hodgekiss's, Herbie thought. "Is Annabelle home?"

"Yes, she's in the yard. Just go 'round back."

"Thanks." Herbie always liked Mr. Hodgekiss.

The boys found Annabelle at the picnic table in her backyard. Herbie stopped to look at the goldfish pond next to the rose bushes. He thought it was neat.

"What are you two doing here?" Annabelle said.

"We brought our two dollars for the class gift."

"It's too late, I already bought the gift after school."

Herbie and Ray sat down at the picnic table. Herbie noticed the class card was on the table next to a box of new crayons and a ballpoint pen.

"I was double-checking to make sure no one signed that wasn't supposed to." She picked up the card. "See, I recopied your poem in neat cursive."

"Hmmmm."

"You can draw something on the cover of the card, Raymond. You are a good artist."

Ray grinned. Then he took a purple crayon from the crayon box.

"I'm sorry, but I paid for the gift already. There's nothing else to get."

Herbie laid the two dollars on the picnic table. "Nothing?"

"Well, we just got the store wrap. The fancy gift box was $1.75 plus tax."

Then she looked at the dollar bills.

And smiled for the first time. "Maybe we can afford to get the fancy gift box now. You boys want to sign the card?"

Herbie grinned.

"Funny thing happened today," Annabelle said as she ruled two lines on the card. "When I went to pick up the ceramic owl at the gift shop, I noticed a big crack in the back of it. It would have broken the first day Miss Pinkham had it."

"What did you do?" Herbie asked.

"Asked for another one, of course. The clerk told me it would be no problem. She said they could get an owl just like the cracked one from their other store. I was going to pick it up tomorrow morning."

"Was?" Herbie noticed Mr. Hodgekiss walking across the lawn. He had that apron on.

"I don't know when I can pick the gift up," Annabelle said. "I have a dentist appointment tomorrow. I'm having my first cavity filled. And I think Martha's House of Gifts closes at one o'clock."

Mr. Hodgekiss leaned on the picnic table. "I don't mean to interrupt, kids, but Annabelle has to eat dinner in ten minutes. I'm fixing eggplant parmigiana."

When he saw the long look on Annabelle's face, he asked, "Is something wrong?"

Annabelle told her father about the problem with the class gift.

"Well," Mr. Hodgekiss replied, "looks like we need a couple of men to do an important job tomorrow." Then he looked at Herbie and Ray.

Herbie swallowed hard. Saturday mornings he and Ray went fishing. Not shopping.

"What do you say, Herbie?" Mr. Hodgekiss asked.

"Eh, sure. We can do it." Herbie didn't want to disappoint Mr. Hodgekiss. "We can pick out that fancy gift wrap easy, right Ray?" Herbie wasn't going to do this *alone*.

"Gift *box*," Annabelle corrected. "The lid is removable." And then she changed the subject. "Either of you ever have a cavity filled?"

Ray looked up from his drawing. "I have. It was

a killer. After the dentist drilled my tooth for an hour, my cheek popped out like a baseball. Took two months to go down."

Annabelle closed her eyes and shivered.

"Course," Ray continued, "that was just in a dream. In real life, it's no biggie."

Mr. Hodgekiss walked back to the house laughing.

Annabelle flared her nostrils at Raymond. "I think you two should sign the card and go. Here's the ballpoint pen. Write your full name—first, middle, and last—here." And she pointed to a special place on the card.

"You want us to write our middle names?" Herbie asked.

"That's what I asked everybody to do."

Herbie noticed the lines she had drawn for Ray and him on the card. "How come you didn't rule lines for everybody?"

Annabelle shrugged.

Herbie knew why. She thought he and Ray wrote uphill and downhill too much.

Herbie took the pen and wrote "HERBERT DWIGHT JONES."

"Dwight's a nice middle name," Annabelle said. "Your turn, Raymond O. Martin."

Herbie leaned over Ray's shoulder to watch, because he had never known what the "O" stood for. It was probably the only thing he didn't know about his best friend.

"Don't laugh," Ray said.

"We won't," Herbie said.

Raymond printed "RAYMOND ORVILLE MARTIN."

"Orville?" Herbie cracked up.

Annabelle giggled, then she stopped when she noticed Ray looked hurt.

"Why Raymond, Orville is a famous name," Annabelle volunteered. She felt bad about laughing at someone's name. It wasn't polite.

"It is?" Ray was curious.

"Haven't you heard of Orville Wright? He invented the first airplane."

"No kidding?" Ray said. "That's one smart dude."

Herbie thought of another one. "I know an Orville who is famous and RICH."

This time Annabelle asked who.

"Orville Redenbacher, the guy who makes pop-corn."

Raymond raised his eyebrows.

"You even look like him, Ray," Herbie added.

"Gee, thanks, Herbie."

Annabelle giggled again.

As the boys got up to leave, Raymond showed the picture he had drawn on the card. It was a Viking ship with twenty-eight oars. Miss Pinkham was standing on the deck with a Viking helmet on her head.

Herbie clapped and whistled.

Annabelle was less enthusiastic. "I like the twenty-eight oars. One oar for each person in the class. That's nice."

Then she took a sales slip out of her cowhide purse. "Take this to Martha's House of Gifts to-morrow around noon. You'll need it to pick up the gift. It has my name on the bottom because I want to be put on the mailing list for future sales. You boys can choose the box since you're paying for it. If I can, I'll meet you there around noon . . . just to make sure everything goes smoothly," she eye-balled them.

Herbie was only half-listening now.

He was thinking about how great it was to have the class gift matter all taken care of.

He and Ray signed the card.

They were a part of the special surprise for Miss Pinkham.

Tomorrow all they had to do was pick out a gift box for the owl.

A piece of cake, he thought.

A piece of cake.

7

The M&Ms Fight

When Herbie and Ray walked into Martha's House of Gifts on Saturday morning, they noticed the pink, thick rug right away.

"Rich place . . ." Ray whispered.

Herbie listened to the music in the store. It reminded him of a dentist's office. Then he remembered Annabelle. He was glad she had called this morning and said she couldn't meet them at noon. Her mother wanted her to take a nap after she had her tooth filled. She said to bring the gift by her house IMMEDIATELY afterwards.

"May I help you?" asked a tall lady with a long skirt.

"Yes," Herbie replied, handing her the sales slip. "We're here to pick up an owl that you sold yesterday."

"Hmmm," the lady said. "I remember seeing an

owl behind the cash register. I wasn't here yesterday, but I know what you're talking about."

The boys followed her to the back of the store.

"Here it is," she said holding it up.

. Nice owl, Herbie thought. "Do you have a gift
box?" he asked.

"We have three kinds of fancy gift boxes. A pink
satin box with hearts on it, a blue paper box with
stripes, or a purple box with white boats."

"The boats!" both boys said at the same time.

The saleslady smiled.

When Ray's stomach growled, Herbie gave Ray
a jab with his elbow.

They watched the lady place the owl face up in
the boat box. Carefully she folded pink tissue paper over it, attached the lid and put the box in a
pink package. "Here," she said.

Herbie reached into his pocket and pulled out
the two crisp dollar bills.

"I just need one," she smiled.

"Just one?" Herbie repeated.

The saleslady nodded. "We have a special on
gift boxes this weekend. Monday we'll be bringing
in a new line."

Ray had a sudden thought. "She just needs

YOUR dollar, Herbie," and he snatched the other one.

Herbie took the package and thanked the saleslady. Then he raced out of the store after Ray.

"What are you doing?" he yelled.

"Man, Herbie, I'm starved. I didn't have any breakfast. Can't we spend this dollar on some candy?"

Herbie thought about it. "Gee, I don't know Ray. That's really the class money."

"Look," Ray said, "we got a gift box that's worth $1.75 plus tax. Who cares if we got it on special?"

Herbie thought about it some more. "The class gift is paid for. The gift box is paid for. What else do we need to buy?"

Ray grinned. "Candy."

The boys raced down several blocks to the drugstore where they had the best selection. On the way, they passed the thrift shop. They noticed a big banner that said "EVERYTHING GOES! CHEAP PRICES!"

"Too bad we couldn't get our candy there," Ray said.

In the drugstore, Herbie and Raymond looked

over each bar, box, and bag of candy carefully.

"I think the giant-size M&Ms is our best bet," Ray suggested.

"Sounds good to me, Ray," Herbie replied.

The boys plopped the dollar down on the counter.

"Too much, boys," the druggist smiled. And he handed them back a quarter.

Ray picked up the M&Ms and the boys headed for home.

"I'll count 'em so we can divide them even steven," Ray said.

Herbie stopped. "I'll count 'em."

Ray shot Herbie a mean look. "Herbert Dwight Jones, I am counting them."

Herbie took a step forward. "Raymond Orville Martin, I AM COUNTING THE M&Ms."

And then Herbie gave Ray a push.

Ray pushed back.

Herbie pushed Ray into a parking meter.

Ray got mad.

He pushed Herbie back so hard that the pink package Herbie was carrying popped out of his arms.

The boys watched it fly into the air, and then land on the sidewalk.

With a clunk.

"Oh no!" shouted Herbie.

"Oh no!" yelled Raymond.

"Look what you did!" Herbie said.

"Me? *You* pushed *me* into a parking meter!"

Both boys dropped to their knees on the sidewalk. Slowly Herbie pulled the gift box out of the package. Carefully he lifted the purple lid. Ray leaned over Herbie's shoulder while Herbie removed the pink tissue paper.

There was the owl.

In hundreds of tiny pieces.

"How could we be so dumb!" Herbie said.

"We're doomed!" Ray replied. "The class will kill us! They expect an owl to come out of this box."

"A twenty-five dollar owl," Herbie added.

Then he took the change out of his pocket and looked at it. "All we have is twenty-five cents. Where are we going to get an owl THAT CHEAP?"

The boys sat on the sidewalk staring at the cracks.

Then it came to them.

They jumped up and ran into the thrift shop.

"It's our ONLY chance," Herbie said.

"It's a real long shot," Ray replied.

8

Owl Be Seeing You

Herbie and Ray walked through the thrift shop. It was a big room. Lots of clothes were hanging on racks. Shoes and belts were in one corner. Furniture was in the back. To the side were shelves of knickknacks.

"That's where we want to look," Herbie said. "Start looking for owls."

The boys combed each shelf. There were cats, and dogs and lots of horse statues.

"I found a neat alligator," Ray said holding it up.

"*Owl*," Herbie said. "It's gotta be an owl, Raymond."

"Couldn't it be an *owl*igator?"

"Nice try, Ray. Keep looking."

After five minutes, Ray stumbled onto something on the bottom shelf. "I FOUND AN OWL! I FOUND AN OWL!"

Several people in the store turned around.

"Shhhh!" Herbie replied. "Where?"

"Here!" He held it up for Herbie to see.

"Wait a minute," Herbie said, "give it to me." Herbie took the ceramic piece and looked at it closely.

"It's an owl, all right. But what's it sitting on?" Herbie felt the grooves on either side of the oval dish. "WHY, IT'S AN ASHTRAY!"

"So?"

"Miss Pinkham doesn't smoke. She HATES smoking. Remember when she showed us that film about a dragon who smoked? He coughed all the time and looked green."

"Yeah, that was neat."

"Well, she wanted us to learn that smoking is BAD. We can't give her this!"

"I still like it," Ray replied. "It looks like it cost big bucks, too, when it was new. I like the owl."

"Forget it, Ray. Annabelle would kill us if we gave the teacher an ashtray. The teacher would too!"

The boys looked in other departments of the thrift store. They couldn't find anything.

Herbie picked up the owl ashtray again.

"Maybe . . . just maybe, if we put something in it, it wouldn't look like an ashtray."

"Like what, then?" Ray asked.

"Hmmm," Herbie mumbled as he bounced an idea around in his head. "The M&Ms! It could be a candy dish!"

"Not the M&Ms, Herbie. I'm starved. I was looking forward to eating those as soon as we got out of here."

Herbie shot Ray a cold look. "We wouldn't be in this situation now if it hadn't been for your stomach. Don't think I've forgotten those Bits O' Chicken!"

Ray didn't say anything.

Herbie held up the owl dish. "We need the M&Ms in this. If they're not in it, it looks like an ashtray. Besides we bought the M&Ms with the class money. They belong with the class gift."

Reluctantly, Ray followed Herbie and the owl to the checkout station. Herbie laid the quarter on the counter and hoped it would be enough.

The lady looked at the item and the shelf it came from. "That's half off. Was one dollar, so now it's fifty cents."

Herbie frowned. They were short.

"That's okay," the lady smiled. "Today, everything goes. It's yours for a quarter."

Herbie beamed.

"Shall I bag it for you?"

"No, we have our own gift box here," Herbie replied.

"How lovely!" said the lady when she saw the purple box with the white boats.

She placed the owl ashtray carefully inside the box. Herbie opened the M&Ms and poured them in the dish.

"Now we can take it to Annabelle's house and she won't know what's inside until Miss Pinkham opens it up on the last day of school."

"What do we do then?" Ray asked as they walked up Main Street.

Herbie started to worry. "We . . . tell her the lady ran out of the kind of owls Annabelle wanted, so . . . so . . . she gave us this one?"

Ray nodded. "Sounds good."

When they got to the corner of Fish and Washington, Herbie was uneasy. "Wait a minute! Annabelle can take the lid off herself. She can see the candy dish now!"

Ray put his arm around his buddy. "No problem, Herbie. We just tape that baby up. We're almost at your house—we can do it there."

Herbie felt a little better, but he said, "Let's make sure we put three rows of tape around that thing.

"And do it neatly," he added.

9

Home Sweet Home

Saturday mornings at the Joneses' were always busy. Mrs. Jones was at the restaurant all day serving coffee and donuts. Mr. Jones had Friday nights and Saturday nights off, so he was up early doing chores around the house. Olivia had to do the laundry and vacuum. Herbie was supposed to take the garbage out, mow the lawn, and make his bed.

As the boys walked into the house, they nearly got strangled by the vacuum cord. Olivia was pulling it clear to the other corner of the room and the cord was very taut. Raymond tripped over it. The vacuum turned off and Olivia turned around.

"You didn't even make your bed this morning, ERB!" That was what Olivia called Herbie when she was angry.

"Why do you think I came back, Olive?" Herbie said.

Ray rolled his eyeballs. He knew why Herbie came back.

"Well, forget it, I already made it."

"Thanks, Olive," Herbie smiled as he walked over to the dining-room desk where his mom kept lots of odds and ends like paper clips, scissors, and nail clippers.

"Here it is. And it's the kind of tape you can see through. Great!" said Herbie. "Let's go to my room and finish the job."

"Speaking of jobs," Olivia interrupted, "you still have the garbage to take out, and the lawn to mow."

Herbie looked at Ray. "No problem. We'll get the garbage right now."

"We will?"

Reluctantly, Ray followed Herbie through the kitchen to the side porch.

"Morning, boys," Mr. Jones said.

They looked up. Herbie's father was sitting on a stepladder, repairing the hole in the ceiling with some new plaster.

"Morning, Mr. Jones," Ray said. "I like your goggles."

"Well," he said taking them off, "sometimes that stuff gets in your eyes. But they're also good for peeling onions."

"Hmmmm." Ray thought he might suggest that to his mom.

"COME ON, RAY!" Herbie hollered from the side porch.

After the boys took out the garbage, they went into Herbie's room and closed the door. They locked it, too.

Herbie sat down on his bed and lifted the lid from the gift box.

Ray looked at the M&Ms in the ashtray. "Do you s'pose those candies are fresh?" he asked.

"Huh?" Herbie leaned forward and smelled the M&Ms. "Smells okay to me. Why?"

"Well," Raymond hesitated, looking at the M&Ms. "Wouldn't it be awful if we gave the teacher stale candy?"

And then he added in a low voice, "Do you think we should try some to make sure?"

Herbie put his hand over the box. "No way, Raymond Orville Martin. I don't trust you when it comes to your stomach."

But when *Herbie*'s stomach growled, Ray persisted. "Just one, Herbie?"

Herbie couldn't stand it. How could one M&M hurt, he thought.

The boys each ate a brown M&M.

"Man, that really hits the spot," Ray said. "I never got breakfast."

"Me either," Herbie said. "Dad had all his plaster stuff on the kitchen counter. I couldn't even make toast."

Herbie pulled some tape off the spool. "Okay let's close the lid."

"Herbie . . ."

"Yes?"

"Do you 'spose those green ones are fresh?"

"Huh?"

"Maybe they made the brown candies fresh, but what about the green ones?"

Herbie looked down at the dish. "What about the red, yellow and tan ones then?"

"Maybe we better taste ALL the colors, . . . just to be on the safe side," Ray said, looking hopeful.

Herbie began to drool.

And then he did it without thinking. He popped a green candy, then a red one and then a tan one into his mouth. As he leaned back against his bed pillow, he thought about the chocolate going down his throat. *Deee*licious. Did he dare have seconds?

When he sat up, he saw Ray tossing a huge handful of candies in his mouth.

"HEY!" Herbie said, jumping to his feet.

And then Herbie did help himself to seconds.

Suddenly, there was a knock on the bedroom door.

Herbie turned. "Yeah, what do you want?" He hated it when his sister bothered him.

"Someone is here to see you."

Herbie's eyes widened. "Who?"

Ray swallowed the last of the red, tan and green candies.

"Annabelle. She's here. Her dad is waiting for her in the car. She came to pick up some gift for the teacher."

Herbie started to shiver. He looked at the one yellow M&M on the ashtray, and shook his head. How could he have let this happen?

"HURRY UP!" Olivia called.

Ray quickly tucked the pink tissue paper over the ashtray and the one M&M. After he closed the lid and wiped some chocolate off his mouth, he said, "No problem, Herbie, just tape it up, quick!"

Herbie wiped some sweat off his forehead, then he reached for the dispenser and started taping the lid once . . . twice . . . and three times.

Olivia banged on the door. "HERBIE JONES, Annabelle's father is waiting."

Herbie held the box up. "What do you think, Ray?" he whispered.

Ray gave him the A-OK sign. "Nobody is going to get that baby open. Not even Miss Pinkham."

Herbie managed a weak smile. Then he put the gift back in the pink package and opened the door.

Annabelle was waiting in the living room. She took the package from Herbie and pulled out the box. "Oh, I like the boats! They go with the Viking ship Ray drew for the class card." Then she looked at Ray's mouth. She noticed the chocolate smeared around the corners.

"You shouldn't eat candy," Annabelle said. "I know, I just came from the dentist. Can you tell I had novocaine?"

Herbie and Ray both shook their heads the same way. First to the left, then to the right.

They were thinking about that ashtray in the gift box, and the one yellow M&M.

"Well," Annabelle continued, "I wanted to pick up the gift myself. It's very important. I wouldn't want you boys to drop it or anything."

The boys stood still.

Like statues.

"Something wrong?" Annabelle asked.

"N . . . n . . . n . . . no," Herbie said with a half-smile.

The boys watched Annabelle walk out to the car that was parked in front of the house.

After they closed the door, they leaned against it and took a deep breath.

"Gee," Olivia said, "you guys look like you're waiting for a firing squad or something."

Herbie didn't say anything. He lowered his head and walked outside to the backyard. Ray followed him.

10

Herbie and Raymond
in Church

Sunday morning early, Herbie called Raymond. He decided to use code language, because what he was talking about was top secret.

"992?"

A sleepy voice replied, "Yeah . . ."

"This is Double 030," Herbie said in a muffled voice. He didn't want his family to hear him.

"What are you calling so early for?"

"I'm gettin' worried about that class gift. Miss Pinkham is going to take one look at that thing and think it's an ashtray. One yellow M&M is not going to make her think it's a candy dish."

"So what do you have in mind?"

"I think we should go to church."

"HUH?

"Listen, Ray, our minister said that when two or

more people pray about the same thing, powerful things can happen. We need help to get out of this mess."

Ray spoke up. "You want me to pray with you?"

"In church. Can you get over here by ten?"

"I don't have a tie," Ray said.

"You can borrow one of my dad's. Just get over here."

At nine-thirty, the Joneses were going around the house shouting.

"Who took my brush?" yelled Olivia.

"Did anyone see my high-heeled shoe?" Mrs. Jones asked. "I looked everywhere."

Mr. Jones sat calmly at the kitchen table, reading the Sunday newspaper and sipping some coffee. He was also admiring the hole he had patched up in the kitchen ceiling.

"MY RED HIGH HEEL!" Mrs. Jones shouted.

Mr. Jones looked under the kitchen table and held up a red shoe in the air. "Is this what you were looking for, dear? I think you were using it last week to make a point. Or was it a heel?"

Mrs. Jones grabbed the shoe. "Do you think this dress is too tight on me? I simply can't eat any more donuts this month. I'm starting to wear them on my hips!"

Mr. Jones put his paper down and pulled his wife onto his lap. "Well, dear, they look better on you than they do in the display case," he said.

Mrs. Jones blushed.

Just as they hugged, there was a knock at the back porch door. As Herbie walked through the kitchen he noticed his parents hugging. Quickly, he looked up at the ceiling. "Nice job, Dad."

Ray walked in. "This okay?" he said as he pointed to his blue suit. "I wore it two years ago when I was the ring bearer in my cousin's wedding."

Herbie noticed his yellow socks showed. "You look fine, Ray. Here." Herbie handed him a brown tie.

"Brown and blue?" Olivia said as she twirled into the kitchen. She was wearing her new dress, the one she wore Friday night to the banquet.

Mr. Jones, who had gone back to drinking his coffee, and Mrs. Jones, who was putting her red high heel on, looked at Olivia.

Herbie looked at his sister, too.

She had on a fancy white dress with a red sash

around her waist. Little red roses were embroidered around the neckline.

Herbie had to admit his sister looked pretty.

But he wasn't going to say it out loud.

"Come on, Ray, I'll help you with your tie."

"No comments?" Olivia said, as she twirled around again.

Mr. Jones put his arms out. "Come here, my little lady."

She ran to her father and he lifted her high in the air.

"Now, Dad, put me down. I'm not a baby any more. I'm thirteen."

"Let's go!" Herbie shouted when he finished straightening their ties. He wanted to get to church and say that prayer.

As the Joneses and Ray found seats in the last row of church, the choir was singing.

When the music stopped, a man in a black robe got up to speak.

"Is that God?" Ray asked.

"No, dummy, that's the minister. God's in Heaven . . . and . . . on earth."

"Well if He's on earth, that means we must

bump into him sometimes," Ray replied.

"SHHHH!" Olivia shushed. "Don't talk in church!"

When the minister held up his hands for prayer, Herbie leaned over and whispered, "Now, remember, we're asking God to help us get out of this class gift mess. Maybe . . . maybe with His help, Miss Pinkham might like the gift."

Ray whispered back, "Should we tell Him we're sorry about fighting over the M&Ms and breaking the owl?"

"Wouldn't hurt," Herbie whispered. "You could also throw in those Bits O' Chicken too while you're at it."

"Let us pray!" said the minister in the black robe.

And the congregation was quiet.

Everyone bowed their heads.

After a minute, Ray sat up. "I'm finished," he said.

"SHHHH!" Olivia said again.

Herbie looked up at Ray. "Think of something else. Just talk to Him."

Ray shrugged and then bowed his head again like Herbie.

When the service was almost over, the minister announced, "And now we will receive your tithes and offerings."

Ray felt inside his pocket. Just one burned-out fuse, he thought to himself.

As a man and a lady with carnations in their buttonholes came up the aisle with a heavy wooden plate, Ray got an idea.

He watched Mr. Jones put an envelope in the plate and pass it to Mrs. Jones. Mrs. Jones passed it to Olivia. Olivia put an envelope on the plate and passed it to Herbie.

Herbie dropped a nickel on the wooden plate, and handed it to Ray.

Ray took off his tie, wadded it up, and laid it on the tray.

The woman who had a carnation in her buttonhole took it without looking.

Herbie leaned over and whispered, "You gave God a tie?"

"Well, your minister said he was collecting 'em."

"Not those kind! He said *tithes* and offerings, Raymond! And that wasn't YOUR tie. It was my dad's!"

Herbie sat back in the pew. He was wondering if bringing Raymond to church was such a good idea.

"Well," Ray said as they walked out of church, "we got to talk to God about that class gift mess."

"Yeah," Herbie said as he put his hands in his pockets. "He knows we need Him, now."

"And you know, Herbie," Ray said, "since I had a little time left, I asked God if He could make the fish bite a little more on Saturday mornings."

Herbie hit Raymond over the head with his rolled-up church program. Then he chased him all the way to the car.

11

Doomsday?

On the last day of school, Thursday, Herbie met Ray at the corner. Ray had a jar of something red in his hand.

"What are those?" Herbie asked.

"Pickled beet slices."

"Pickled what?"

"Beet slices. Mom buys them all the time. She says they can be partyish, too."

Herbie rolled his eyeballs. He was glad his mother was not like Mrs. Martin.

"What did you bring?" Ray asked.

"Annabelle signed me up for punch three weeks ago. So that's what I'm bringing for today's class party."

"What kind?"

Herbie's face broke into a smile. "Adam's Ale."

Raymond stopped walking. "YOU BROUGHT A WHOLE GALLON JUG OF WATER TO OUR PARTY?"

Herbie nodded.

"I don't believe you, Herbie."

"Well, it's true. We're not buying soda this week at my house. Mom and I made a deal about that."

Ray started walking again. "Well, right after Miss Pinkham sees my great picture, and reads your great poem, we cut out the door, right, Herbie?"

"Yeah . . . unless . . ." Herbie looked up at the rolling clouds. ". . . unless our prayer worked."

"I don't know," Ray said. "I think He's too busy to think about an ashtray."

"You're probably right, Ray. Plan on hightailing it out of there with me."

When the boys walked into the classroom, Annabelle was putting fresh daisies in a vase on Miss Pinkham's desk. The class gift was placed right next to the class card on the teacher's green blotter.

Herbie stared at the purple box with the white boats. Why did they have to drop it? It could have been so perfect.

Herbie plopped down in his chair and put his gallon jug on the reading table next to Ray's pickled beet slices and Margie's chocolate chip cookies.

Annabelle came right over to him. "Oh, Herbie, I am so thrilled about our class gift, I can't wait. Can you? Hmmmmmmmmmmm?"

Herbie grumbled something.

"Why Herbie, you seem mad. Something bothering you, hmmmmmmmmmmm?"

Annabelle's "hmmm"s were starting to bother him.

John Greenweed came in the room with a giant plastic bag of popcorn. Phillip McDoogle brought a package of paper cups.

"Glad you brought a gallon jug of punch, Herbie, popcorn makes me thirsty," John said as he set the popcorn down.

Herbie smiled. Wait till they taste my Adam's

Ale, he thought.

A moment later Miss Pinkham walked into the classroom.

Herbie stared at his teacher. He had never seen her look so beautiful. Usually her blonde hair was pulled back in a wooden barrette. Today, she let it fall to her shoulders. She had a blue suit with a white blouse and little blue raindrop earrings.

Herbie looked out the window. He wished he had stayed home sick.

His moment of doom was coming. But first, he had to hear Miss Pinkham read the poem he had written for her.

"What's all this?" Miss Pinkham said as she saw the present and card on her desk.

Annabelle stood up immediately. "It's a gift for you . . . from the class."

"My goodness! How thoughtful! How did you plan all this without my knowing about it?"

Annabelle replied, "It wasn't easy." She was thinking about the time she had to stay after school.

Miss Pinkham picked up the card. "What a wonderful Viking ship. Did Raymond draw that?"

Raymond stood up. "I sure did. Do you like the

helmet I put on your head?"

"Oh!" Miss Pinkham replied, "Is that me?"

"You're the captain."

Miss Pinkham laughed. "I love it! How thoughtful you were to draw this, Ray."

And then she opened up the card and saw all the names. "How nice that you all wrote your full names."

"That was my idea," Annabelle said softly.

Miss Pinkham smiled, "What a nice idea, Annabelle."

"And look at this poem. Did you write it, Annabelle? It looks like your handwriting."

"No," Annabelle said. And she didn't volunteer who did.

Herbie sat still. He was hoping someone would tell Miss Pinkham. He felt funny telling her himself.

"Then it must be Herbie Jones," Miss Pinkham said. "Am I right, Herbie?"

Herbie sat up straight. "You're right," he beamed. She knew his writing style. She was the one who first told him he was a good writer.

Everyone listened as Miss Pinkham read the poem aloud:

This is a rhyme
At the end of the year
To say you are nice
  And sweet.
Enjoy your vacation—
Read some good books,
Sit down and
  Put up your feet.

Miss Pinkham pulled a Kleenex from the box on her desk. Herbie could tell she was going to cry.

"This card is a gift all by itself, boys and girls. I love the drawing, the poem, and the way each one of you wrote your full name. I will treasure this. It is really from the heart."

Herbie wished that had been all the class had given her. She seemed so pleased with just the card.

Herbie edged off his chair and got ready to leave.

"What a precious box!" Miss Pinkham said. "I love the boats!"

Herbie watched as she lifted the lid off. It came off easily.

Why?

He had taped three rows of tape around that thing. He leaned over and pulled on Annabelle's dress. "You took the tape off?"

Annabelle reached for her cowhide purse and opened up her wallet. "I have something for you, HERBERT DWIGHT JONES."

"Huh?" he motioned to Ray to wait a minute. Ray was ready to run out the door.

Miss Pinkham removed the tissue paper.

Annabelle handed Herbie one yellow M&M.

"YOU KNOW!" Herbie said, sinking down in his chair.

Miss Pinkham pulled the tissue away.

Herbie looked up at the teacher. She would hold up the ashtray any moment now.

Ray had his head down on his desk.

Herbie got ready to run.

"HOW BEAUTIFUL!" Miss Pinkham exclaimed.

BEAUTIFUL? Herbie thought to himself.

BEAUTIFUL? Ray thought as he raised his head off his desk.

Miss Pinkham held up a ceramic owl. It was the same owl that had broken into a hundred pieces.

"What?" Herbie said out loud.

"Shhhh! I'll tell you later, Sleazeball."

"How did you know I collect them? This owl is just wonderful!"

Herbie couldn't believe it.

The owl was the one that he had bought at Martha's House of Gifts.

Ray looked over at Herbie and mouthed the words, "IT WAS A MIRACLE!"

"Boys and girls," Miss Pinkham said, "thank you so much! I will keep this owl always, just like the card."

"Now, let's PARTY!" John Greenweed said, as he passed out his popcorn.

Annabelle turned toward Herbie. "I can't *believe* you actually put an ashtray in that gift box for our teacher!"

"Where is the ashtray?" Herbie asked.

"Martha's House of Gifts called me that same night to apologize for giving us the wrong owl."

"The wrong owl?"

"The one with the crack in the back. It was lucky I filled out the bottom part of that sales slip with my name and address. She was able to get in touch with me. After I went down and got the owl,

I came home and opened up your gift box. I was shocked!"

Herbie breathed a sigh of relief. Miss Pinkham was happy with her gift.

Annabelle continued talking, "I was just lucky that I didn't have to return the owl with the crack in it. The sales lady said she didn't want it. So I took that awful ashtray and threw it in our trash."

"Why didn't you tell me before?" Herbie asked.

"Because I wanted you to suffer. You deserved some punishment for trying to pawn off a used gift like that on our teacher!"

Herbie sat back in his chair. It was over!

"Popcorn?" John Greenweed said to Annabelle and Herbie.

Ray came rushing over to Herbie.

Herbie knew he would need to explain everything to him.

And it would be a pleasure, he thought.

Miss Pinkham had got her class gift and the class card with HIS poem on it. And she said she was going to keep it always.

"I'm thirsty," Annabelle complained. "Who was supposed to bring the punch?"

Herbie smiled. "I was. May I pour you some?"

"Why, Herbie Jones, your manners are improving."

Ray stood back and smiled while Herbie got the gallon jug.

Herbie held it up. "It's called 'Adam's Ale.'"

"What a wonderful name. Is it like ginger ale? I love that."

"No, it has a taste of its own. I think you can best appreciate it if you close your eyes when you drink it."

Annabelle closed her eyes.

Herbie placed the cup in her hands.

Annabelle took three quick swallows, and then made a face. "HERBIE JONES!" she yelled, "YOU BROUGHT WATER TO OUR END-OF-THE-YEAR PARTY!"